This book belongs to _____

Library of Congress Cataloging-in-Publication Data

Zöller, Elisabeth, 1945- author.
[Antonia, die mit den Pferden flüstert. English]
Antonia, the horse whisperer / Elisabeth Zöller and Brigitte Kolloch; with illustrations by Betina Gotzen-Beek; translated from the German by Connie Stradling Morby.
  pages cm. -- (Rosenburg Riding Stables ; volume 1)
Originally published in German by Coppenrath F in 2011 under title: Antonia, die mit den Pferden flüstert.
Summary: «Antonia loves horses but when a skiddish gelding arrives at the stables--who only responds to Antonia--will she be able to keep him safe until his French owner comes to check on him?»-- Provided by publisher.
ISBN 978-1-62636-383-0 (hardback)
[1. Horses--Fiction. 2. Horsemanship--Fiction. 3. Human-animal communication--Fiction.] I. Kolloch, Brigitte, author. II. Gotzen-Beek, Betina, illustrator. III. Morby, Connie Stradling, translator. IV. Title.
PZ7.Z74An 2014
[Fic]--dc23
                              2013035686

Elisabeth Zöller & Brigitte Kolloch

Antonia,
the Horse Whisperer

The Rosenburg Riding Stables, Volume 1

Illustrations by
Betina Gotzen-Beek

Translated from the German by
Connie Stradling Morby

Sky Pony Press
New York

For Ever and Ever

She had won the big jumping competition! A no-fault ride with the best time! No faults!

Antonia was absolutely stunned and overwhelmed. She sat on Snow White, her horse. The gray mare pranced with excitement and seemed just as proud as Antonia.

Yes, she, Antonia Rosenburg, had actually won first prize in the horse show!

"The result of years of training . . ." she heard a voice exclaim over the loudspeaker.

He means us, Snow White and me, she thought, and enjoyed the resounding applause. She stroked Snow White's mane, stretched, then lifted her head and swung it, shaking her long hair to the back. Her eyes lit up with joy. She could hardly believe it. They had won! And the people in the stands were clapping for her.

Next to her Leona was sitting on Thunder. Leona, her very best friend. Had she won too?

"Man, I knew it," whispered Leona. "You and Snow White cleaned up all the prizes!"

Somewhere in the audience Antonia's father, Alexander, and Grandma and Grandpa Rosenburg were sitting. And, of course, her older sister Caroline was there too.

Antonia bowed her head as the medal was hung around her neck and then she accepted a gleaming trophy. A ribbon was placed on Snow White's bridle. Proudly, Antonia sat up straight in the saddle and waved to everybody. The fanfare sounded, and the six best riders galloped their victory lap for the grand finale. It was a wonderful feeling. It was like a dream . . .

. . . from which she suddenly awakened, because somebody was calling to her. What had happened?

"Hello!" Leona leaned down toward her from the top bed and grinned. "You were talking in your sleep again!"

Antonia rubbed the sleep from her eyes and beamed. "Really? I was standing on the very top. It was an unbelievable feeling!"

"Antonia, you've gotten to the top so many times.

You know the feeling already. I train and train and I'm still not half as good as you. You were just born to ride horses." Leona jumped out of bed and pointed out the window. "It's going to be a super-duper day! Not a wisp of a cloud to be seen. Riding and swimming are on the menu today!"

And the sun really was shining brightly already, sending its warm rays into Antonia's room. Antonia stretched her arms and legs. Yes! It would be a great day. It was summer vacation! Finally! Six weeks of riding, swimming, and dreaming.

"Get up!" shouted Leona.

Antonia leaped out of bed. She would be able to spend the whole day with her best friend and Snow White. And tomorrow, too. And the next day. Leona was staying here at Antonia's house, in her room, for three weeks. That's what both friends had wanted for their summer vacations.

Antonia suddenly felt butterflies in her stomach. The Snow White butterflies! Today was Snow White's big day; today, she finally got the bandage off. At last Antonia and her mare would slowly be able to begin training again. But there was another feeling, too, a slight ache in her tummy and a nervous trembling. Was it doubt? *Oh, nonsense. Everything will be fine*, Antonia told herself.

"We're going to the lake after riding, right?" Leona was such a tomboy! There wasn't a sport she didn't try. And that's how she looked: slim, well-trained, short-cropped blonde hair, blue eyes, and thousands of freckles on her snub nose. Swimming and riding were her absolute favorite sports, and she was really good at swimming and best at diving. Antonia was sure one of Leona's ancestors must have been a real mermaid.

Antonia liked to swim, too, but really, for her, there were only horses. She had been sitting on horses since she was barely able to walk.

Below in the farmyard, Felix and John, the two grooms, were puttering around already. On the Rosenburg stud farm, things started early—at six o'clock; otherwise, horse care, stable care, riding and jumping, feeding, and stall mucking would never get done. The little tractor rumbled over the path. Mr. Rosenburg used it to distribute feed. Antonia's father was usually the first one out in the morning and, as the feed specialist, he gave each horse its "breakfast helping," as he lovingly called it, shortly after six o'clock. Meanwhile the grooms mucked out the stalls and groomed the horses.

Antonia and Leona slipped into their clothes. Now there was no holding them back. Downstairs in the kitchen, they heard Karen clattering the silverware. Karen Steinmann was the good fairy in the house and ran the big household with Grandma, while Antonia's father, her aunt Maria, and her grandfather took care of the horses, breeding, stables, and riding lessons.

Antonia's mother was no longer alive. She had died when Antonia was only three years old. Sometimes it made Antonia sad that she could barely remember her. When she felt that way, she would run to Grandma or Caroline, who would tell Antonia about her.

But this was no time for sadness.

"First, to the horses!" called Antonia. "And then we'll pack our breakfast and ride to the lake." During vacation, she and Leona were always in the barn, accompanied by Bellmondo, the lively Bernese mountain dog. He leaped around their legs, ran ahead, waited impatiently for the two of them, and let them give his head a scratch.

Antonia took a deep breath of the still fresh summer air. Yes, here she was at home; her room was in the big longhouse, exactly over the huge kitchen, whose big bay window gave a clear view of the old oak tree. In the back part of the longhouse were twelve of the twenty-five stalls in which cows and pigs had once lived.

Last year, the newer stalls had been incorporated into the former coach house across the way. And Grandma and Grandpa lived in-between in the "sheepfold," as they lovingly called their little half-timbered house, in which sheep really once were kept. There they were entirely separate from the main house and lived right in the middle of the busy horse farm.

Antonia and Leona opened the big gate to the stables. The sweet smell of hay greeted them, as well as the warmth and familiar lip-smacking and neighing.

"Hello, Fiona. Hello, Morning Star. Hello, Mr. Right. Hello . . ." They greeted the horses left and right—the gray horse, the brown ones, the black horse, and the sorrel; they heard snorting, kicking, and the sounds of impatient horses waiting for feed. Antonia's father divided the hay portions evenly; the doors behind them stood open, and the tractor rolled up from there.

"Hello, Thunder!" called Leona, stroking her favorite horse.

It was through Thunder that Antonia and Leona had met. Three years ago, Leona's parents had looked for a good stable for Thunder and for a riding instructor for Leona. The Rosenburg Farm was the best farm far and wide, and Leona was instantly impressed by the friendly atmosphere.

"There are really terrific horses here!" she had shouted with joy, and then, as Antonia came around the corner, the two had immediately become friends. From that day on, the two girls were inseparable.

Antonia went three stalls farther to Snow White. "Snow White, hello! How are you?" An affectionate snorting and familiar neighing were the answer.

"You've been waiting for me, right?" Antonia stroked down Snow White's back to her legs and carefully touched her bandage.

"That's coming off today," she whispered in Snow White's ear. "And then you have to be patient. We have to take it easy at first. But we'll be fine." She looked at the tight bandage, which had been supporting Snow White's hind leg since the fall exactly six weeks ago.

"Of course, you'll start with long rides around the Rosenburg Farm, but I'll just lead you at first," Antonia whispered to her. "You'll see, it's changed a lot in six weeks. The grain fields are full of blue cornflowers and red poppies. They finished building the new indoor riding arena. There's no scaffolding anymore. You'll like it. And Grandma's rosebushes are blooming as beautifully as ever!" Snow White seemed to understand every word and answered with a vigorous snort. "We won't go to the jumping area until much later."

Antonia held out a few oats for Snow White. "But this will be the last morning with this annoying bandage." When Snow White had eaten her oats, Antonia led her to the grooming area, put her grooming kit down, and began to run the soft brush over the horse's neck and back. Snow White held completely still while she was brushed; only a soft, melodic humming came out of her nearly closed mouth.

"See, the sun is shining. From now on, we'll be

outside again every day. It's the perfect time to slowly get moving again." Antonia patted her mare's back and flanks, combed her mane and tail, removed pieces of straw from the comb, and ran the soft brush along her legs. With the hoof pick, she cleaned Snow White's hooves.

"And now for a little treat, my dear," she exclaimed cheerfully and went back to the stall with Snow White.

She heard her father, who was approaching a car that had just rolled into the farm. Voices came closer. Grandpa accompanied Mr. Rosenburg and Dr. Kemper, the veterinarian, to the stalls. Dr. Kemper had been there so often in the last weeks. He had shown Antonia everything she had needed to know about splinting, bandages, and other dressings. Today, finally—after six long weeks—the nightmare was over.

They greeted each other with a nod, and Antonia relinquished her spot in the stall to Dr. Kemper. Good thing the stalls were so big after the renovation last year! Her father and grandfather had planned it well. Now she was able to stay there during the examination and look comfortably over Dr. Kemper's shoulder. Dr.

Kemper set down his portable ultrasound unit in front of the stall. Leona waited there anxiously with Mr. Rosenburg and Grandpa. The three of them looked through the bars.

Dr. Kemper opened his bag and got a syringe ready. Was that some kind of sedative shot?

Get on with it, Antonia thought impatiently. Her eyes looked at him imploringly. Dr. Kemper greeted Snow White, petting her ears and tail. At last he bent down.

As the vet slowly loosened the bandage, Snow White flinched.

"Snow White, easy. What's the matter?" Or was Antonia mistaken? That shouldn't be painful anymore! But once Dr. Kemper had completely removed the bandage, a noticeable shudder ran through Snow White's body. Was she trembling in pain? No, it was just relief. Dr. Kemper got the ultrasound unit. Grandpa, Antonia's father, and Leona looked at the screen too. Unfortunately, Antonia couldn't see a thing from her corner of the stall.

The adults looked serious. For goodness' sake,

what did that mean? Why was Dr. Kemper shaking his head? Six weeks, he had said back then, and they were up today. The veterinarian stared ahead for a second, almost self-consciously, then looked from Mr. Rosenburg to Grandpa and finally at Antonia. Even though he wasn't saying anything for the time being, Antonia knew exactly what he would say to her.

As though through a bank of fog, she heard Dr. Kemper explain, "I'm sorry, Antonia, but you won't be able to jump Snow White anymore. At most, you can go for a little ride."

Alexander Rosenburg pulled Antonia toward him and took her under his arm, and Grandpa put his calloused hand on her shoulder, as if he could protect Antonia from everything bad.

Dr. Kemper was speaking again, and Antonia forced herself to listen to him. "The chances weren't good from the beginning. It's true everything is healed, and with careful, specific exercises, she could be pain-free. But jumping is no longer an option. Never again. Further therapy, even complex operations in the animal clinic, won't fix that. You know, it was an eighty percent tendon tear, which exhibits a poor tendency to heal. With easy movement on firm ground and with supportive, conservative therapy, Snow White can slowly be ridden again. But this kind of healing process drags on for many months. The scar tissue is much less elastic and can't withstand the intense pressure of jumping. However, Snow White will soon be fit again for quiet rides."

Antonia heard everything from afar, understanding nothing and not wanting to. Tears ran down her face. Snow White was her friend. They had done everything together up to now. She turned and ran out of the stable. From a distance she heard Leona call, "Wait, Antonia!" But she just kept running—through the hens clucking around, scattering under protest. Tears clouded her vision, and she couldn't see where she was running. From behind, someone laid a hand on her shoulder, and Leona whispered, "Antonia, come back. Snow White needs you. Surely she understood everything and is just as sad as you."

"So what?" sobbed Antonia. "It doesn't matter." She stuck out her lip defiantly.

"You're just disappointed now, Antonia. But Snow White needs you, really. She realizes that something's wrong. You have to comfort her."

Antonia nodded; Leona gave her a nudge, and they headed back to the stable. Mr. Rosenburg, Grandpa, and Dr. Kemper had left. It was just Antonia and Leona now.

Antonia took Snow White's head in her hands. She stared at the mare for a while. "You'll be my friend forever and ever. I promise."

She whispered it twice, like an incantation, then repeated it loudly the third time. She wanted everyone to hear it. Snow White was her friend!

And Snow White looked at her so lovingly that she felt sick again. She pressed her head on Snow White's neck and sobbed while Leona gently rubbed her shoulder.

Just this morning I had this fantastic dream that I was standing on top as the show jumping winner, thought Antonia. *Will that ever happen now?*

Out of the Dream

The next day Antonia scanned the big pasture. Where was Snow White? She swept her dark brown hair out of her face and closed her eyes. Very softly she whistled through her fingers. Right away she heard a familiar neighing—just as usual!

Antonia felt footsteps approach on the soft ground. Her gray mare came limping happily up to her.

"Hey, old girl." Antonia smiled and carefully removed a few burrs from Snow White's light coat. "Here, my dear," she whispered softly and held a carrot out to the horse. Warm air streamed out of the mare's soft nostrils.

"Oh, Snow White." Ever so slowly, Antonia became conscious of the thought that she would never again be able to jump Snow White. But she still wanted to be a show jumper! She wanted to be just as successful as her mother once was and as her older sister was now. Before Antonia was born, her mother had won every competition that had a high status and reputation. Antonia, along with Leona, had often looked at the old videos and photo albums of her mother's competitions. Doing that always made the two friends start daydreaming. Antonia's mother looked so happy and proud in the photos. Antonia wanted to experience the same feeling.

But then the horrible accident had happened. Her mother had died instantly. Antonia's father was sad all the time and didn't want to do anything. Caroline slowly snapped out of her grief, and Grandpa and Grandpa moved into the sheep stall. Shortly thereafter, Maria, Papa's sister, came to live with them. Maria had said right from the beginning that she didn't want to—and couldn't—replace their mother, but she had consoled both children and given them new strength and confidence.

Antonia still remembered it all clearly.

She had just turned three years old and had called out so many times for her mama. And although Maria had come to her bed and Papa had stroked her head, and although Grandpa had sung songs and Grandma had read stories to her, Mama never came.

Whenever she thought about her mother, Antonia felt an emptiness that made her feel helpless and endlessly sad.

Nobody had been able to console her—with the exception of Snow White, who, in her warm, soft way, had filled a little part of this emptiness with life.

After that, everything had been okay. Antonia felt as if she were one with Snow White. More and more she wanted to intensify the jumping instruction and improve her skills.

"Please don't put so much pressure on yourself, my girl," Papa had said. "You're still just a child."

"It's okay," Antonia had answered and laughed. "For me, there's nothing better than practicing with Snow White." And as often as she could, she disappeared into the riding ring to set up the cavalettis. A few months ago, Grandpa and Grandma had given Antonia a book about the height-adjustable hurdles.

Since then, Antonia and Leona had read a lot about cavaletti drills and had tried them out. It was so much fun! Caroline was a specialist at it already. And because of that, Antonia tried especially hard not to miss a practice with Caroline. Her sister was awesome; she could learn a lot from her.

On her horse Rush On, Caroline moved almost serenely in the saddle. Her jumps were so elegant, as though nothing could be simpler. Caroline would sit in absolute harmony with Rush On, erect on his back, smiling at Antonia and Leona, and a second later she would be completely focused on her horse and the next jump.

Together with Mr. Sonnenfeld, Antonia and Leona had devised a detailed training plan of their own. First, with the help of the cavaletti drills, her horse's muscles would become limber and free of rigidity in order to build up more muscle. And Thunder, Leona's lively Arabian gelding, got more relaxed and stronger day by day. Snow White had also looked forward to every lesson. Until that day, six weeks ago, everything had been wonderful.

Again and again, Antonia thought back to that horrible day. It was a Sunday morning. Antonia had arranged to meet Leona in the outer paddock. They wanted the quiet of the morning for a training session, before visitors or the owners of the other horses came, as happened so often on weekends.

Leona was on time, as usual. On this Sunday, however, she ran to meet Antonia, extremely upset.

"Snow White!" she shouted, out of breath. "Snow White is hurt! I was just riding my bike along the pasture and was going to say hi to her. That's when I saw it. Come quickly!"

Antonia and Leona ran to the fence. There stood Snow White, thrashing her head back and forth in panic, her eyes wide with fear. Immediately Antonia saw that Snow White's right hock was extremely swollen.

She kept lifting her leg painfully in order to take the pressure off it.

What had happened? Yesterday they had done two easy jumping exercises, but afterward, when Antonia had curried and brushed her, everything had been fine.

"Easy," said Antonia, caressing Snow White's nostrils. She stroked along her leg, ran her fingers through her mane, and pressed her head into her neck. "Snow White, sweetie," she whispered. She had to calm herself too. Antonia had an enormous lump in her throat, and her heart was pounding. Once more she carefully felt Snow White's leg.

She must have overlooked something. She tried to recall the individual jumps from yesterday. Had Snow White not taken off correctly one time? Or had she gotten caught on a hurdle? Had she been injured that way?

Snow White was trembling. Antonia stroked her back and belly. Was she shaking from pain or was she just agitated?

Antonia took a step closer to Snow White so she could whisper soothing words in her ear. Then the horse's foot slid into a deep hole.

Antonia was horrified. "That must have been it! Snow White stepped into this stupid hole, all nicely overgrown with grass, but very dangerous."

Everyone knew that holes like that should never be in meadows where horses were kept. Every evening, Antonia inspected the meadow thoroughly with John and Felix. Where had this hole come from?

At that moment, the sound of barking echoed over the meadow. Antonia grumbled, "There, listen to Trix; he's chasing horses again. He probably dug the hole and, of all things, it had to be Snow White who stepped in it. My poor baby, come here. Oh, Snow White!" She stroked the horse's neck. At that exact moment, the neighbors' dachshund, Trix, came around the corner, eager to run through the meadow.

Antonia stormed up to him and grabbed him by the collar. "Out!" she said firmly, pointing with her outstretched arm toward the neighbors' property.

Head hanging low, Trix trotted away. He should

know that he had no business here.

"That horrible dachshund . . . " Antonia shook her head and hurried back to Snow White. Even though she thought she knew how the accident had happened, it didn't make anything better. The horse was still hurt.

Gently, Antonia leaned her head on Snow White's neck and stroked her back. She always liked that a lot. They stood there that way for a while. When Snow White had calmed down, Antonia put on the halter that Leona had fetched.

"Will you help me get her back to the farm?" Antonia asked Leona. Bravely and with a number of pauses, Snow White limped with both girls to the Rosenburg farm.

A little later, Antonia's father had called the veterinarian.

"A tendon tear," Dr. Kemper had said after a thorough ultrasound examination. Then he had explained what that meant. Antonia could have screamed.

Even now, sitting on the fence and stroking her carrot-chewing horse, it still shook her up, just like it had on that horrible day. Snow White snorted softly and nudged Antonia gently with her soft nose.

A few days later, the sisters were playing Scrabble. Antonia couldn't concentrate and didn't form a single word.

"What's the matter with you?" asked Caroline, laying her hand tenderly on Antonia's arm.

"I did everything wrong," sighed Antonia. "Crud." Frustrated, she swept the letters off the table.

"Now you're being crazy, sis," Caroline snapped at her. "Stop, already. You didn't train her wrong, you didn't dig the hole—none of that. It was an unfortunate fluke," she said somewhat more gently. "You explained about the hole and Trix."

Easy for Caroline to say; she had it all: her horse, her jumping, her success. Although there were enough horses on the farm, Antonia didn't want any of the others. She didn't even accept Leona's offer to go for a ride on Thunder.

Caroline didn't ease up. "Look, Antonia. If you really want to be a show jumper, you'll have to get used to a new horse more than once. For example, Snow White was just right for you as a first horse." She looked at Antonia in a very adult-like manner. "But Snow White wasn't a good jumper from the beginning. You would have had to look around for a new horse soon anyway."

"You're so nasty," Antonia interrupted her.

But Caroline didn't get worked up. "And even with the new horse, it won't last," she said, unfazed. "Because the better you get, the better your horse has to be. That's the way it is if you ride jumpers and want to

advance. Many of the most famous riders have several horses they train and take to competitions." She put her arm on Antonia's shoulder and dragged her into the living room where their mother's trophies and pictures stood on a bookshelf.

"See here? There Mama's riding on Abadi, and in the background Papa is holding Bagira's reins. This picture," she continued, pointing to a gold-framed photo, "is from three years later, and Mama is riding on Cairon." Caroline's voice grew softer. "You can believe me. Mama loved her horses as much as you love Snow White. Of course, you have to establish a close relationship with your horse. But you also have to be able to leave it at some point for another. That's the way a rider's career usually goes. Closeness and good-byes and closeness, time and time again. And in-between are riding and jumping."

"And loyalty," Antonia added.

Caroline nodded. "Yes." She gave Antonia a big hug. Then the girls strolled across the farm. At times like these, Caroline was the best sister in the world. Antonia looked at Caroline from the side. She was three and a half years older than Antonia. Antonia wanted to be as pretty as Caroline someday. Caroline was a head taller than she was, slender, and already had a real bust. When she wasn't riding, she always wore her long brown hair down—it fell in light waves over her shoulders and framed her narrow face.

Just then, Aunt Maria rushed up to both girls along with Leona, who jumped off her bike, completely out of breath.

Aunt Maria stood in front of the three of them and gushed, "You won't believe it. The famous French show jumper, Marcel Bonhumeur, is going to leave three of his horses with us for a few months."

"Is he the one with the stable near Paris?" asked Caroline. When it came to horses, she knew everything! She read every horse magazine she got her hands on; and when riding allowed her some free time, she also looked up more information about riding on the Internet.

"That name was easy for me to remember because it's so cheerful: Bonhumeur means 'good mood,' doesn't it?"

"Exactly," said Maria, laughing. "And Marcel Bonhumeur has really good horses. If he leaves his three treasures with us for a few months, it's a big break for the Rosenburg Farm!" Maria told about how she had first bought Elfin Dance for Mr. Bonhumeur at a white-knuckle auction and then later found Cascara and Asseem for him at another stable.

"Elfin Dance—the name is like a magic spell," whispered Antonia.

"Marcel Bonhumeur," Maria reported, "is a real big shot in the riding business, a patron of quite a few well-known riders. He's the CEO of a big firm and gave up competitive riding. He hardly has time to ride any more, but horses mean the world to him. No matter how good-natured he seems, with his eyes as round as marbles and his little belly, and no matter how humorous his name sounds, he can get nasty when something happens to his horses! So, the greatest care is called for when he boards them here. Only our employees are allowed to look after the horses. John and Felix will ride them and, of course, Mr. Sonnenfeld. Nobody else! There will even be a contract that includes that. But isn't this wonderful! They're coming to our Rosenburg Stables. It's news that is sure to spread!"

Since 1758, the Rosenburg Farm and Stable had been in the possession of the Rosenburg family. A moat still ran along the backside; up front it had been filled in. In summer, fragrant roses surrounded the farm, which had originally been a moated castle.

The building looked like a castle, with towers, oriel windows, and a heavy wood entry door. Antonia's great-grandparents had added on the longhouse, with its wonderfully ornate gables. It was so roomy that they could live in it as well as keep horses.

The von Rosenburgs were a proud family. Antonia's father had long since given up the "von" in his name because he said that today you shouldn't have nobility in your name, but rather in your heart. Grandpa, however, had protested and kept his "von."

The Rosenburg family had always bred horses on the side. But Antonia's father wanted more than that. Together with his sister, Maria, he wanted to make the Rosenburg Farm a place for exceptional horses. For that reason, they had employed Mr. Sonnenfeld, who had previously been a jockey at the Berlin racetrack. And that meant something. Maria was the one who evaluated, bought, and sold the horses. She had a good feel for horses and a long-practiced eye, so that she immediately recognized the animals' strength and elegance.

She had stood by her brother and said, "Let's make something really good out of our old Rosenburg Farm. I'll take care of the horses. We'll make an upscale stable. And you'll be the principal riders."

With that, she had hugged Antonia and Caroline.

Maria was small and fine-boned, with short hair and sparkling brown eyes. Since Maria had moved in with them, she had brought them a new sense of hope, even if the path they wanted to take had many obstacles. In the meantime, one famous animal or another had been housed at the farm, but the big breakthrough was missing . . . until today.

That's why Maria was so excited about the prospect of Marcel Bonhumeur's horses. She hugged Antonia and Leona, talked incessantly, raved about the three horses, and clapped her hands. Maria was more of a friend than an aunt and wasn't much taller than Antonia. She had such an easygoing way about her that she infected everyone with her enthusiasm and joy.

At first, Antonia hadn't been able to get used to the idea that Maria would be living with them at the Rosenburg Farm. Until then, she knew her aunt only through her once- or twice-a-year visits. Otherwise she traveled all over the world, traded valuable horses, went to competitions and stud farms, and attended auctions.

"When are the horses coming?" Antonia asked.

"I expect them tomorrow, at about this time. Could you both please go have a look with John and Felix to see if the new stalls at the back are in shipshape form?"

John, who was doing his apprenticeship as a groom, rode across the farm just then. When he saw Maria with the girls, he gushed, "Have you heard? Three top horses for us. Now we'll have to hustle and clean stalls!"

Maria laughed.

John headed for the row of stalls.

Felix, a very good rider himself, arrived just then and called after John, "Make sure they are immaculate!"

"You got it, Chief," replied John. He knew that would irritate him. Felix hated it when John, who was only three years younger, called him Chief.

Love at First Sight

The next day the time had come. In two hours, the precious cargo was to arrive. Certainly Mr. Bonhumeur wouldn't be there for the delivery of the horses—he intended to come to the Rosenburg Farm sometime later—but the people delivering the horses had his complete trust; they would see to the terms of the contract and pass on their impressions to Mr. Bonhumeur.

So, despite the heat, the farm bustled with activity. Everyone knew exactly what needed to be done. John and Felix, along with the girls, had cleaned all the stalls, Grandma was baking a cake, and Grandpa was straightening up the office for the tenth time. Everybody was hoping that with Mr. Bonhumeur boarding his horses here, the Rosenburg Farm would finally be seen far and wide as an exceptional stable.

Aunt Maria suddenly slipped Antonia a small package. It was a tiny wrapped gift.

Maria often brought back something for Antonia and Caroline from her trips. Antonia ripped the paper off immediately and opened the box; a little elf charm made of rose quartz lay inside. Wasn't one of Mr. Bonhumeur's horses named Elfin Dance? Is that why Maria had bought her the pendant? But before she could ask, a whistle sounded across the courtyard and a silvery, sparkling, elegant horse trailer drove up to the farm. Everyone lined up quickly. As both horse handlers jumped out of the driver's cab, they were greeted with loud hellos. They looked around the Rosenburg Farm admiringly and nodded their approval.

Maria promised to show them around after the horses had been transferred to the stable.

Finally the tailgate was lowered and Cascara stood impressively on the ramp. She was dark and fiery, with a black mane, and only her white coronet markings gleamed. Cascara raised her head and whinnied a friendly greeting to everyone.

"Come, girl." Felix approached her, carefully took the reins, led her down the ramp, and walked with an almost ceremonious stride to the stables.

A second horse—Asseem—climbed majestically down the ramp. Now the Rosenburgs nodded in admiration. That was a horse! John welcomed Asseem, who approached him elegantly. Asseem had a completely spotless coat, a round white faint star on her forehead, and a black mane and tail.

Then came the third horse—a long-legged chestnut gelding with a stripe. He neighed wildly, performed a dance, rolled his eyes, and repeatedly avoided Mr. Sonnenfeld's slow attempts to get close to him. Mr. Sonnenfeld talked softly to the gelding and patted his neck and flanks, but the gelding would not calm down. Maria sprang toward him; John and Felix also wanted to help, but Mr. Sonnenfeld held them back.

"Quiet, there, there," he said over and over. The horse threw its head back and forth wildly.

"That must be Elfin Dance," said Antonia's father.

Antonia, who was standing a little behind him, observed the horse intently: a skittish, brown bundle of energy, defiant as a little child, powerful, and surely very fast. He also had a wildness that wasn't consistent with his elegance.

And as if automatically—later she wouldn't have been able to say why—she called very gently, "Elf-in Dance!" It was almost a singsong. She called once again, softly, but clearly, "Elfin Dance!"

And then Elfin Dance stood still, listened to the gentle words, turned on the spot as if he were looking for the owner of the voice, and met Antonia's gaze!

Antonia stopped, thunderstruck.

"Are you my friend?" she wanted to whisper. Instead she said, "Come," and, with a questioning look at her father, who nodded affirmatively, took the reins as if it were the most natural thing in the world. Together with Mr. Sonnenfeld, she led the horse in the direction of the row of stalls. She knew for a fact that she wasn't techni-cally allowed to take care of Elfin Dance—that was Mr. Sonnenfeld's job. But she had barely let go of the reins when Elfin Dance reared up. He looked at Antonia reproachfully and refused to budge from the spot.

"Go to him and stay with him until he's in his stall," murmured Antonia's father. Elfin Dance pranced, and she took the reins once again. Slowly she went with him toward the stalls.

"I'm here, Elfin Dance," she whispered. "Welcome to the Rosenburg Farm, you beauty."

Her hand stroked his neck and finally stopped, staying calmly on his cheek. Antonia felt a great strength well up inside her, something irrepressible. She looked at him at length.

"We'll get to know each other," said Antonia, already knowing that she had found a new friend.

Leona rubbed her nose. She always did that whenever she was excited.

Only Grandpa shook his head. "That won't be possible. Mr. Sonnenfeld is responsible for Elfin Dance. It's in the contract."

But nobody was listening to Grandpa; it was as if everyone stood dazzled by the beautiful horses that had just arrived.

Guilty Conscience?

In the middle of the night, Antonia awoke with a start. The lighted numbers on her alarm clock read 3:20. She had to go to Elfin Dance. This magical moment, a vision in a dream, had struck her once again like lightening. She had to go to him. . . .

Very gently she pushed the blanket aside and climbed out of bed. She tucked her sandals under her arm, crept to the door, and prayed that none of the floorboards would creak and wake Leona. She had to get to the stall—had to make sure that everything was all right with Elfin Dance. After all, it was his first night in a strange place!

Antonia knew well enough that she had better not get caught. All she had to do was go down the stairs, open the terrace door softly, and then she would be outside.

She ran across the farm to the stables, and there stood Elfin Dance! Big and gorgeous. He was completely calm and relaxed and just looked at her with his beautiful dark eyes. And yet Antonia felt his wildness and strength as she carefully approached him and softly stroked his neck. She wasn't afraid. It was just the opposite; she felt an unusual joy and great trust, although she knew absolutely nothing about him. How had Elfin Dance been broken in? How did he prefer to be ridden?

Then Antonia heard a soft snorting coming from the rear stalls. That was Snow White! Instantly Antonia felt guilty. What was she doing? She had run directly to Elfin Dance and hadn't even greeted Snow White! Her mare needed her too! After greeting Snow White affectionately, she crept back to bed.

Nobody had seen her, and back in the room, Leona seemed to be sound asleep and dreaming. Antonia couldn't fall back to sleep, though. How could she have simply run past Snow White? And what about Elfin Dance? She knew she wasn't allowed to take care of him or to ride him. And yet, she had been the only one the temperamental horse had listened to when he arrived. She had seen Grandpa's worried face. Certainly he was wondering how they were supposed to care for Elfin Dance if he didn't learn to trust John, Felix, and Mr. Sonnenfeld. And there was the agreement they had to follow.

That afternoon, Antonia and Leona sat in the grass and watched Caroline practice jumping. But Antonia, who usually watched Caroline carefully for tips, couldn't concentrate at all.

"What's the matter with you?" asked Leona, taking a bite of Grandma's yummy chocolate cake. "Did you sleep all right?"

"No, not enough sleep," grumbled Antonia, and then she told Leona about her nighttime outing. After all, girls tell their best friends everything. "Can you believe that I didn't think about Snow White at all or even say hi to her? And a few days ago I swore my eternal friendship to her. I feel like a traitor!"

"So what?" Leona laughed. "It doesn't make you a traitor. Nobody can help falling in love with Elfin Dance. He's a dream horse," she raved. "He's a bit too temperamental for my taste, though. He's only a gelding, but you have him under control. By the way, Cascara and Asseem aren't from bad parents either."

"That's for sure," said Antonia. And the thing about the breeding was true too. Maria had already explained to Antonia a lot about breeding and good ancestry. As a rider, you had to know those kinds of things.

"But with Elfin Dance it's different. It's as if we've been friends for ages. If I'm honest, even last night I was able to imagine jumping him." She twisted her hair around her index finger nervously and scratched behind her ear. Immediately her guilty conscience came back. "But I can't do that to Snow White," she murmured.

"I think," said Leona, "you shouldn't worry about Snow White so much. Don't you think you can love two horses at the same time? The way you love your dad and Maria? Or cake and chocolate?"

Now Antonia couldn't help but laugh and added, "Like swimming and riding?"

Leona continued, "Right. Or candy and bubble gum. Christmas and Easter. Vacation and weekends."

"Snow White and Elfin Dance!" Antonia shouted as she touched her little elf charm in her pants pocket.

"Exactly. Now you've got it." Leona giggled and clapped her hands. "It's so sad you can't jump Snow White anymore. But with Elfin Dance you'll be the best show jumper in the world."

"Well, that's probably an exaggeration. Anyway, that's only a dream. That dumb contract says that I'm not even allowed to touch Elfin Dance, let alone ride or jump him! Only Mr. Sonnenfeld is allowed to handle him." All at once Antonia lowered her voice. "Luckily, Mr. Sonnenfeld promised me that I could slip into Elfin Dance's stall now and then, but only when Grandpa isn't around. If Grandpa catches me with Elfin Dance, then—"

"Your Grandpa has to be strict," said Leona. "A contract is a contract. Otherwise, why would you make one?"

"We have to come up with a way for Elfin Dance to stay here, so you'll be allowed to ride him," Leona said later. Broodingly she laid her right forefinger on her nose and knit her brow. She always did that when she was hatching some crazy idea. And she was a world champion at that! "Can't you just buy Elfin Dance?"

Well, this idea was more than crazy!

Antonia had to laugh. "Yeah, sure. Mr. Bonhumeur will definitely be satisfied with the little bit of money I have in my savings if I ask him for Elfin Dance! Horses like that cost a lot, like thousands! I can't afford that–and neither can Papa, Grandma, and Grandpa combined. You'd better come up with another idea." She twisted a lock of hair around her forefinger.

"Okay," Leona thought some more. "How about if you cast a spell on Elfin Dance? You talk to animals so well. Just whisper into Elfin Dance's ear that . . . "

She didn't get any further because all of a sudden the two girls heard a horrible noise coming from the riding stable, and then somebody screamed for help.

Help!

Leona dropped the cake from her hand in shock. Bellmondo ate it up with a cheerful wag of his tail. Both girls jumped up and ran in the direction of the stable. They found Mr. Sonnenfeld sitting on the ground in front of Elfin Dance's stall. Mr. Sonnenfeld was holding his forehead and groaned softly, "Oh my goodness . . . "

Mr. Rosenburg came running in with Maria.

"What happened?" shouted Maria, but really all anybody had to do was take a look at Elfin Dance. The horse was neighing loudly and rearing up continuously.

"I just wanted to feel his pulse," said Mr. Sonnenfeld in a shaky voice, "because I suspected that he had caught a cold on the trip here. It's not beyond the realm of possibility—first the fully air-conditioned trailer and then out into this awful heat . . . but he wouldn't let me anywhere near him and reared up right away. At the last second I was able to get out of harm's way. He

did give me a little whack, though. He's a wild thing."
Mr. Sonnenfeld finally smiled. Then he happily let Mr.
Rosenburg help him up. He was limping a little. He
looked as though he had sprained his ankle.

"You lie down for a while, put ice packs on your forehead and ankle, and I'll go get a doctor," said Antonia's father, supporting Mr. Sonnenfeld as he walked. Antonia took a deep breath and then exhaled loudly. She had been scared to see Mr. Sonnenfeld sitting on the ground. He was a lot older than her father. And he had taught her so much over the years, including how to be calm when dealing with horses and how to have the patience to keep starting over when things weren't going as planned. Mr. Sonnenfeld was always a source of encouragement to her.

While Antonia was still trying to calm down from what she'd seen, Maria slowly approached Elfin Dance. If Mr. Sonnenfeld suspected that Elfin Dance might be sick, she definitely had to check him out. Mr. Sonnenfeld was rarely mistaken in his assumptions, and Maria was worried about what would happen if Mr. Bonhumeur came to the farm in a few days and found that one of his horses was sick. Elfin Dance let Maria into the stall. When she went to touch him, however, he recoiled and threw his head back and forth, neighing loudly. He did not rear up, but Maria knew that if she pressured him further, the same thing might happen to her as it had to Mr. Sonnenfeld.

"Antonia," Maria called softly so that Elfin Dance didn't become agitated again. "You try it. Talk to him. But be careful. Don't get too close to him." Maria opened the stall door and let Antonia in, ready at any moment to step in front of her for protection. Leona watched the scene through the stall's bars as if spellbound!

But Antonia wasn't afraid. She spoke to Elfin Dance, approached him slowly, and looked at him. Immediately he stopped snorting and stood still.

"Elfin Dance," Antonia whispered to him. "What's the matter with you? You scared me, you wild thing! Mr. Sonnenfeld is my friend, and he was just worried about you. You have to be a little nicer." Antonia talked and talked, finally stroking Elfin Dance's head, and then felt for his pulse. Twenty-eight to forty beats per minute was normal, but Elfin Dance's pulse was racing! She felt his jowls. Was it a fever? Mr. Sonnenfeld was right! The horse was sick.

Maria sent Leona to the house. "Call Dr. Kemper. Even if it's just a little cold, he should see Elfin Dance."

Leona ran off and returned five minutes later. "Dr. Kemper's coming in an hour. Mr. Sonnenfeld's ankle is so swollen that he has to go to the hospital to get it checked out. In any case, I'm supposed to tell you that he won't be able to take care of Elfin Dance for at least a little while."

Antonia and Maria looked at each other, perplexed.

"Now what?" asked Antonia.

"Very simple." Maria was all smiles. "You'll take over Elfin Dance's care until Mr. Sonnenfeld is able to

again. You're the only one Elfin Dance listens to anyway."

Antonia couldn't believe her ears. "Me?" she said. "You want *me* to take care of Elfin Dance?" She excitedly threw her arms around her aunt's neck. But suddenly she fell silent. "What about Grandpa? He'll never allow us to break the contract."

"Well, Grandpa is right. But we still have to come up with some way to take care of Elfin Dance," answered Maria. "Maybe I should just get in touch with

Mr. Bonhumeur and ask him what we should do?"

But would the horse's owner really entrust the care of such a valuable gelding to a ten-year-old girl?

"Mr. Bonhumeur doesn't know you're a horse whisperer," Maria continued, "and something like that is hard to explain. He will have to see it."

The Plot

An hour later, Dr. Kemper drove onto the farm. Antonia and Maria stayed with him in the stall, and Elfin Dance submitted to the examination calmly.

"You were right, Antonia," praised Dr. Kemper. "Mr. Sonnenfeld's hunch about a cold was right. It will be gone in three to four days."

He gave them a powder that had to be mixed into Elfin Dance's food.

"Keep a close eye on Elfin Dance," Dr. Kemper said as he was leaving.

"Easy for him to say," said Antonia. "Papa, are you sure that Grandpa has to know that I'm taking care of Elfin Dance?"

"I'm afraid so," answered her father. "We have to tell Grandpa. We certainly can't keep it a secret from him that you're caring for Elfin Dance. And he won't exactly be happy about it. A contract is a contract.

And if we let Mr. Bonhumeur know that our caregiver is sick, that won't make a good first impression either. And I'm sure he won't approve of a ten-year-old taking over for Mr. Sonnenfeld." It was a real predicament.

Alexander Rosenburg took his daughter by the hand, and they sat down on a straw bale. His voice became thoughtful and also a little sad as he said, "Your mother had the same gift as you. She could also calm the wildest horses with just her voice. At first I couldn't imagine it, but then I experienced it firsthand. Grandpa doesn't believe in that sort of thing—horse whispering, I mean. He thinks it's nonsense, even though he's seen what you were able to do when Elfin Dance arrived here—and also what your mother did."

Antonia's father paused for a moment and looked over at Elfin Dance, who seemed to be following every word with pricked ears. "We've waited so long for a really good contract. It's very important that Mr. Bonhumeur's horses get the best care here."

"And if it doesn't work out?" asked Antonia.

Her father just shook his head in answer.

That evening, when it wasn't so hot any more,

Antonia wanted to take Snow White for a little walk around the farm.

"Come, my dear. I'm warm, too, but you need a little exercise for your leg. Afterwards you'll get a cool shower, I promise." Snow White didn't really seem to want to walk, so it didn't surprise Antonia when the mare stopped in front of Elfin Dance's stall. But then she stuck her muzzle through the bars and snorted softly. Elfin Dance turned, saw Snow White, and answered with an equally soft, almost tender neigh.

"Hey, you two, do you like each other?" Antonia was happy and let them stand together for a while

as they nuzzled and sniffed blissfully. But finally she pulled Snow White along by the reins. She led her past the new indoor riding arena and then past Grandma and Grandpa's house.

"What are we going to do?" she heard Grandpa ask through the open window. "Poor Mr. Sonnenfeld won't be able to work for three weeks. John and Felix will have to take care of that wild thing. I'm too old for this stuff!" Antonia debated for a moment whether she should keep on eavesdropping.

"What do you think about Antonia helping them take care of Elfin Dance?" asked Maria. Antonia wanted to jump for joy.

But Grandpa replied, "Antonia is only ten years old. And with such a valuable horse? You can't be serious!"

Disappointed, Antonia reached for Snow White's reins and grabbed at nothing. Suddenly Antonia heard a heart-rending scream from the porch! She barely had the porch in view when she stopped in horror. Grandma had planted herself in front of Snow White, who was calmly eating her rose bushes! Blossom after blossom disappeared into Snow White's mouth. One bush had already been destroyed when Antonia raced forward and grabbed Snow White by the mane. "Are you crazy, Snow White? You can't eat Grandma's roses!"

But Grandpa, who had been drawn outside by the noise, came to her rescue. He stroked Antonia's head and said with a mischievous smile, "Antonia, I'm glad that you're taking such good care of Snow White, but rose blossoms are really a bit too much! Look, one of the bushes is bald already." Everybody laughed, and Snow White neighed happily. Whew, this time Antonia had gotten off easily.

Early the next morning, Antonia ran to her father in the stable. She greeted Felix, who had just stuck his head under the hood of the tractor to clean the air filter.

"I've got it, Papa!" she yelled to her father from a distance. "I have a super idea! We should stable Snow White in the stall next to Elfin Dance! Then I'd be near both horses and Grandpa won't notice exactly which horse I'm taking care of. He's not in the stable that often anyway. And I'll only go for a ride when Grandma and Grandpa aren't here. What do you think?" Antonia looked at her father expectantly. When he didn't immediately agree, she pulled out another card. "Besides, I'm very sure that Snow White and Elfin Dance will like each other. Yesterday they sniffed each other for a long time. Maybe Elfin Dance will get calmer having her nearby."

Finally her father was convinced. "Well, then, let's get started with the move. But, Antonia, as far as going for a ride on Elfin Dance is concerned, that's off limits for now. We'll have to discuss that later."

Two riding students were scraping manure up from the floor with pitchforks, so Antonia had to raise her voice. "Okay, I won't ride. Promise. But you really shouldn't help with him, Papa. You have so many other things to do. I'll do it with Caroline and Leona."

John, who had just gotten fresh hay from the hayloft and had overheard the conversation, called from the ladder, "I can help, too, Mr. Rosenburg."

"All right, but when you need me, let me know. And

as far as Elfin Dance is concerned, be very careful around him! Horses are bigger and stronger than people."

"Understood," Antonia reassured her father and began looking for Leona and Caroline. The four of them, working together, quickly had the stall next to Snow White's ready. Almost ceremoniously, Antonia, along with John, led Elfin Dance to it. Snow White neighed as she saw her new neighbor. Right away the two horses stood at the bars separating them and sniffed each other. Leona watched, wide-eyed. "They like each other," she observed in surprise. "It's just like they are best friends."

"They have a crush on each other," Antonia giggled.

Antonia's father, who had joined them again, asked, "When you've gotten through with that, could you two help curry and exercise the other horses?"

"Sure, Papa." They got to work right away. Antonia checked in on Elfin Dance from time to time. His pulse was still too fast, but Antonia would be sure to monitor him continuously—and of course check in on Snow White too!

As Antonia and Leona were laying in their beds that

night, Antonia sighed. "Hopefully everything will go well with Elfin Dance and Snow White."

"I'm sure it will," answered Leona, yawning.

"There is nothing nicer than living on farm like this," Antonia continued.

And Leona agreed before falling fast asleep.

The Storm

For three days, Antonia and Leona took care of Elfin Dance and Snow White. If she and Leona hadn't been staying in the same room, Antonia would have moved into the stable with her sleeping bag and pillow to attend to the horses night and day. But that's where Leona had drawn the line.

"Antonia, don't flip out over this. Elfin Dance has a little cold. He's not deathly ill. And Snow White is running around happily. Besides, the two of them are next to each other—they're snuggling their noses together as though they were a couple." Both girls had to giggle again.

It really had been a super idea to put the two horses together. Every time Grandpa came into the stable, he thought Antonia was caring for Snow White; and Elfin Dance and Snow White liked each other so much that Antonia felt extremely happy watching them stand together, muzzle to muzzle.

On the fourth day, Dr. Kemper said that Elfin Dance was healthy again.

"You should keep him busy now, Antonia. This bundle of energy definitely needs to move after being forced to rest for three days," said Maria. Then she added, "You must promise, though, that you won't take him out for a ride and that you won't leave the farm. Maybe you can try lunging him first. That calms many horses.

"You'd better stay on the course, too, otherwise it's too dangerous. Leona, Caroline, or John should always be nearby in case Elfin Dance rears up and throws you off. And watch out for Grandpa!" Grandpa, thank goodness, was away a lot these days.

Antonia followed Maria's instructions for several days. Elfin Dance slowly became more and more used to her. At the same time she wanted more than anything to ride him in the open field. Maybe if Papa came along she could? Or perhaps even Felix or John? Then she could try to take a real ride! She begged and begged and also showed her father how well she and Elfin Dance got along with each other in the riding arena. Finally, she got him to agree, but only if Felix came along as well.

When Leona and Caroline heard that, they wanted to come too, so an hour later, they all left the farm together. They first rode into the woods. The ground was soft and gave way under the horses' hooves. Antonia sat lightly in Elfin Dance's saddle.

"This is a dream!" she shouted as she felt Elfin Dance's forward-thrusting strength under her.

Her father rode ahead of her and Felix behind. They continued on over the fields at a gallop. Leona and Caroline could hardly keep up because Elfin Dance was so fast. Even though he was headstrong, he responded to the slightest pull on the reins or squeeze from Antonia.

Antonia happily spread her arms out for a moment and sucked in the warm and heavy afternoon air deeply.

"Tomorrow we'll jump a few rounds," promised Caroline as they made their way back to the Rosenburg farm. "I'll set up the hurdles soon."

The group hadn't even reached the farm before Maria came up to meet them. She was very upset, waving a letter in her hand. Sweat was running down her brow as she called to them, "Marcel Bonhumeur is coming tomorrow! Marcel Bonhumeur is coming tomorrow!"

Antonia didn't understand Maria's agitation. Everything was all right. Elfin Dance was healthy again; she had taken good care of him, after all. And Cascara and Asseem were doing really well.

But then it came to her in a flash. "How dumb am I?" She hit herself on the forehead. And all of a sudden she broke out in a cold sweat! Of course, *she* had taken good care of Elfin Dance, but not Mr. Sonnenfeld, who was really supposed to have looked after him. Supported by a crutch and wearing a thick bandage, he'd been limping around the farm since yesterday, and mounted on Elfin Dance, he would not make a good impression.

Despite the heat, Antonia's whole body was trembling as she climbed down from Elfin Dance. She, Leona, and Caroline rubbed the horses dry, cleaned their coats and hooves, took the animals back to the stable, and gave them what they needed for the night. Now all they could do was hope that the next day everything would miraculously go well. None of them knew how they should handle the meeting, least of all Maria. Maybe Antonia could stay near Elfin Dance so that he'd at least remain calm? But as soon as the idea came to Maria, she rejected it.

Antonia and Leona didn't sleep all night. They stayed awake, not just out of concern for the upcoming visit, but also because the warmth and increasing mugginess had become more and more unbearable. There wasn't even the slightest hint of a cool breeze. Then suddenly a flash of heat lightning interrupted the darkness. Something was brewing, laying heavily on them, but it didn't storm and the heat just intensified.

Not until the next morning did threatening black and sulfur-yellow clouds gather in the sky. Today of all days.

"I cannot believe this," said Maria, distraught. An ever-approaching rumble could be heard, and the heat blanketed Rosenburg Farm like a sauna. Everyone knew how nervous horses could get in severe storms. Whenever there was a storm, all farmhands were constantly busy calming the animals, rubbing them dry again and again, and encouraging them by talking. They longed for the first crack of thunder to sound.

"But please, don't storm at the exact moment that Mr. Bonhumeur pulls in," sighed Maria. "Please, please, not then . . ."

All the hard work they'd done on the farm for all these years was now in danger of being destroyed by all these unfortunate circumstances.

But the heat shimmered on and on mercilessly, and the little black storm flies settled in everywhere. The horses swished their tails, their skin itched, and they stamped in their stalls. John, Felix, Leona, Caroline, Antonia, and Maria had already spread out a whole mountain of towels that were damp from drying off the horses.

The increasingly oppressive heat bothered everyone, but it was the most uncomfortable for the horses. They either dozed, incapable of moving, or woke with a start, jumping wildly and hitting the doors as if, with their keen instinct, they were sensing the still distant thunderstorm's approach.

Then finally, around noon, Mr. Bonhumeur drove up. The waiting was over. But despite his name, Mr. Bonhumeur seemed to be in a bad mood already as he climbed out of the car. Was it also because of the heat?

Maria led him around the Rosenburg Farm, showing him the modern stalls, the new indoor riding arena, and the show jumping course. She did this with great composure, although Antonia sensed her tension. Maria was used to giving a big performance at auctions

71

and competitions, so she chatted cheerfully.

Mr. Bonhumeur looked everything over wordlessly. Again and again he wiped his face with a huge colorful handkerchief. "Zees ees really zome 'orrible weazzer," he moaned.

At last he asked to see his horses, whom he'd actually never laid eyes on before.

John and Felix came riding up from the stable on Cascara and Asseem. The horses pranced nervously. Again and again they pricked their ears and threw their heads back and forth. The dreadful stormy air made them jittery and easily startled. There was nothing to be seen of their usual very self-assured and powerful demeanor. Mr. Bonhumeur was quite taken with the elegance of the horses nevertheless.

But then came Mr. Sonnenfeld on Elfin Dance. Antonia held her breath, stayed near both of them, and tried to maintain eye contact with the gelding.

Mr. Sonnenfeld tried his hardest, but it was obviously difficult for him to ride with his injured foot. He sat stiff in the saddle, like a beginner who was afraid of falling.

It was almost like a comedy routine. But the whole business was much too serious for that. Elfin Dance had his ears pricked, and the whites of his eyes were clearly visible. He was looking at Antonia now. But again and again he kicked his hind legs and turned around and around, as if he could possibly get rid of his clumsy, annoying rider. Maria swallowed and fiddled with her handkerchief, and Papa gave a little cough. Antonia really just wanted to jump out in front of Elfin Dance and help calm him.

Mr. Bonhumeur stood there with his mouth open. "Mon Dieu," he shouted over and over, obviously an-

noyed. What was he supposed to think of such a performance? He was used to witnessing the best riders on the most elegant horses.

And when Antonia went up to Elfin Dance and whispered calming words in his ear, that was the last straw for Mr. Bonhumeur.

Once again he yelled, "Mon Dieu, what ees zees? Zose are zuh trainers of my valuable 'orses? Such fantastic stables and zenn such 'orsemanship? And, ma petite girl, get away from zat 'orse! You are just making 'eem nervous!" And he waved his hands as if Antonia were a pesky fly. "Tomorrow I am taking my 'orses from zees farm back to Frahnce."

Maria and Mr. Rosenburg intended to reassure him. But before they could, the thunderstorm let loose with a deafening racket. Antonia had never experienced anything like it. The sky was pitch-black, and fat raindrops—then sheets of rain—pelted down. It was as though someone had opened a floodgate. Lightning flashed, and at the same time, a huge clap of thunder boomed over the farm, as if it wanted to knock the house and stable down. Again and again lightning sliced through the sky, which was black as night, and that's when chaos ensued.

At the last second, Felix and John had been able to jump off the horses' backs before they reared in panic.

Mr. Sonnenfeld, however, could hardly hold on. He thrust Elfin Dance's reins into Antonia's hand and waved John closer, grimacing in pain.

"You two take over," he shouted, and Antonia's father immediately rushed to help.

Mr. Bonhumeur ran back and forth with no idea of what to do, yelling, "My 'orses, my expensive 'orses; take care of my 'orses! And get zees girl away from my 'orse. I weel be so 'appy when we go back tomorrow to Frahnce!"

Felix managed to handle Cascara and Asseem, but when Mr. Bonhumeur tried to snatch Elfin Dance's reins roughly from Antonia, he got the shock of his life!

The gelding reared up, neighed wildly and loudly, rolled his eyes, and galloped away. Neither Antonia, John, nor Mr. Bonhumeur could hold him.

"Elfin Dance!" Antonia called after him. "Elfin

Dance, stay here!" And she ran after him as far as the meadow. He stopped then with his head up.

Antonia could faintly hear Maria telling Mr. Bonhumeur soothingly, "Let them be, Mr. Bonhumeur, and don't worry about it. Nothing will happen to Elfin Dance."

As if in slow motion, Antonia approached the excited gelding. Impetuously he ran from right to left, thrashing with his head and snorting loudly.

"Easy does it, my dear. It's just a storm, and it will stop soon. You don't have to be afraid. I'm with you. Just come to me," said Antonia in her musical voice.

She repeated this over and over until she finally got through to Elfin Dance. He pricked his ears and trotted up to Antonia. Antonia took his reins and continued talking to him soothingly. The gelding reacted to her words and stood in front of her, as focused as if the storm were already far away. John stood behind Antonia.

Now, in order to calm Elfin Dance, Antonia began to lead him around slowly in a circle, as if lunging. And every time a flash of lightening split the dark clouds, or thunder rolled, she spoke to him all the more urgently.

And throughout it all, Elfin Dance walked around in a circle. In a steady voice, Antonia told him everything that was happening. She spoke to him as she would have spoken to a little child, and Elfin Dance walked to the rhythm of her words.

Antonia's wet hair fell in thick strands onto her face. Her T-shirt and riding pants were also stuck to her.

At last, the storm slowly moved on. The thunder was just a distant grumble now.

Elfin Dance's coat, wet with rain, shone like silk as one of the first gentle sunbeams pushed through the clouds. An almost ghostly quiet lay over everything. Or was it soft, fluttering fear? But fear of what?

Would Mr. Bonhumeur take Elfin Dance away with him? Would Antonia lose her new friend? She didn't even want to imagine what else would happen when word got around that Rosenburg Farm didn't properly look after the horses in its care. How many riders would then remove their horses from the farm? She also knew that she'd miss Elfin Dance. The gelding had grown on her so much.

Elfin Dance got nervous once again. But he listened closely to Antonia's words and stood still in front of her after one of his laps.

"Elfin Dance," said Antonia, taking his head carefully between her hands, "my big boy, my wild child!"

Elfin Dance pranced again on the spot, finally calming himself down.

Maria approached cautiously and gave Antonia a big, dry towel. Elfin Dance briefly averted his gaze. Eventually he nudged the towel in Antonia's hand with his mouth, as if he wanted to say, "Now rub me dry."

Antonia took it and stroked carefully over Elfin Dance's head, back, flanks, and then farther down his legs. At last, she threw the towel over him, because she knew he liked it.

A slight tremor passed through his muscles and Elfin Dance let her stroke his crest. Antonia ran her hand over his forehead, nostrils, and jowls. "My good boy," she whispered. "Now we're slowly going to go home."

She took his reins and led him back to the farm. Maria and Mr. Bonhumeur were waiting.

"Magnifique," murmured Mr. Bonhumeur. "Antonia, show me 'ow you would ride heem."

There was nothing else Antonia would rather have done. She adjusted the girth, while Elfin Dance turned to her and almost tenderly stroked her arm with his nostrils.

Then she gently swung onto his back.

It went fabulously. She rode a few laps; he jumped easily over the ditch; they changed the pace. Elfin Dance's talent and temperament were apparent with each step—he pressed forward and was able to demonstrate his strength and ease in every little jump.

"He's something really special," whispered Maria, "and has such elegance."

Mr. Bonhumeur looked him over with a big smile.

"Antonia," he began softly. "Antoinette ees a—'ow do you say—merveilleuse rider, and Elfin Dance ees a character, oo la la!"

"Marvelous," said Maria.

"Antonia ees a magician." And for the second time he smiled. "Zuh girl ees a magician like my Juliette, a real miracle."

Maria was happy. She knew that Mr. Bonhumeur had a daughter named Juliette, who was about the same age as Antonia.

"Yes, really," he repeated. "Eet ees a miracle."

"Antonia, the horse whisperer," said Maria.

"Zat ees right," he answered. "Antonia, zuh 'orse whisperer." And after a pause, he tapped his head and added, "We 'ave to do somezing, mademoiselle. We must zink it over. A plan ees developing; eet ees developing in my 'ead, oo la la."

All's Well That Ends Well

The next day the sun shone brightly. It climbed over the red roofs of the Rosenburg Farm and bathed everything in its warm radiance. Even though it seemed like it would be another hot day, the air was clear and felt pleasant after the storm.

Just like every morning, the stable bustled with activity: feeding, mucking out, grooming, and riding. But it all seemed more relaxed and cheerful than usual.

Antonia and Leona had slept deeply. They had fallen into bed dead tired after the excitement of the day. The storm had raged on for quite a while. It had taken some time after that before the horses settled down and all traces of the storm were gone. Even Mr. Bonhumeur had vigorously pitched in. It wasn't until late, after he had made sure his darlings weren't lacking anything, that he left the farm and had gone to the hotel where he was staying. "I weel come again tomorrow morning and we weel talk wiz more peace and quiet? Somezing must be done. I 'ave a plan," he said before leaving, tapping his head again.

"I wonder if he'll really take Elfin Dance, Cascara, and Asseem back to *Frahnce* with him today?" Leona said as they sat at breakfast. Antonia laughed at her imitation of Mr. Bonhumeur. "All horses get scared in that kind of storm. As somebody who knows horses, he must be aware of that. And besides, he saw how well you got along with Elfin Dance."

Leona rubbed her itchy nose. Was that a sign?

"Yes," answered Antonia softly. "But I'm just ten. He won't leave his valuable horses with a ten-year-old just because I was able to calm Elfin Dance yesterday."

At that moment, Mr. Bonhumeur drove onto the farm and was immediately welcomed by Maria and Alexander Rosenburg. Then, at his request, he was taken to the office. Grandpa came along as well, and the door closed behind the four of them.

"What do you suppose they're talking about? Hopefully Mr. Bonhumeur isn't bringing legal action against Papa for breaking the contract."

"Nah," said Leona soothingly, "he definitely won't do that." She rubbed her snub nose, which was red by now. "I just have a feeling about it. He talked about a plan."

"What kind of plan is that supposed to be?" Antonia sputtered, almost furious. She was on edge. If Elfin Dance was taken away from them . . . only now did she realize how bad that would be. At that instant, she touched her little elf charm in her pants pocket. Was it a sign? Oh, nonsense, it was a piece of rose quartz and nothing more.

Antonia and Leona walked toward the stable. "As long as the four of them are hunkered down in the office, this is probably the last chance I'll have to say good-bye to Elfin Dance," said Antonia. She had been imagining what it would be like to train Elfin Dance, especially now that Snow White was no longer able to

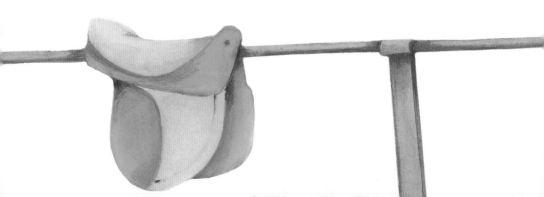

compete. But would she ever get used to riding another horse? If it was Elfin Dance, then yes! Most certainly! With him, she could imagine being able to achieve her dream of a career as a show jumper.

All of a sudden Leona was clinging to her arm. "Hey, we'll just kidnap Elfin Dance. What do you think?" Did Leona really mean that, or was she just trying to cheer Antonia up with one of her crazy ideas? Antonia wasn't sure, but, after a moment of confusion, she had to grin. Leona was always able to help take her mind off of difficult situations.

"And exactly where should we take him? To your house or to the garage?" That thought made both of

them giggle.

"Yeah, it's not a bad idea. And then the newspaper will say, 'Horse kidnapped. Where did the evil kidnappers take it?' And suddenly there will be neighing coming out of our garage."

"Just picture it. We'd have to bring hay and concentrated feed to your house on our bikes. That would hardly attract attention in town. Old lady Mueller would crouch behind her drapes and get all wide-eyed. Then she'd have something new to gossip about at the hairdresser."

"We could bury the horse poop in the garden. That would be good fertilizer for Mama's lettuce and for the flowers. Every stinking piece of horse poop would grow into a fat, fragrant blossom."

"And so that Elfin Dance would have air and light we'd open the door to the garden at the back of the garage."

"All of a sudden a horse would be in the garden. Papa would stare in amazement and call the fire department, and Jonathan would say, all laid-back, 'Hey, there's a horse in the garden. Does anybody recognize him?'" That made them both laugh so loudly that John and Felix looked over at them with quizzical expressions.

Then Antonia became serious again.

"Yes, that would be lovely. I just think that Papa has enough on his plate. A kidnapped horse would be the last thing he'd need."

"Look, here come the reinforcements!" shouted Leona as they saw Mr. Sonnenfeld and Mr. Hegemann enter Mr. Rosenburg's office. Mr. Hegemann was a well-known show jumper who had a big stable in the neighborhood and many times he had trained on the Rosenburg Farm or had a horse trained there. Papa had dreamed about collaborating with Mr. Hegemann for a long time, but it had remained only a dream.

"Maybe the horses are going to Hegemann's," Leona guessed.

"Don't be silly. Mr. Bonhumeur wants to take them back to France," Antonia said worriedly. She sighed. What did Mr. Bonhumeur intend to do with the horses? He *had* spoken of a plan. Was it something good or not? He had been so unfriendly when they first met.

Still, at the end of the day, he had become conciliatory and had even praised her for her ability to calm Elfin Dance. Antonia didn't know what to think any more. No, Mr. Bonhumeur would not leave Elfin Dance with them. In the end, she was just a little country bumpkin to him, nothing more.

Leona put her arm around Antonia. "Look, now we'll finally know more for sure . . ."

The office door opened; then closed again. Nothing happened. The door stayed shut for quite a while.

"Geez, how long are they going to keep sitting in there?" groaned Antonia three hours later. Was it so difficult to convince Mr. Bonhumeur that it had been necessary to break the contract because Mr. Sonnenfeld had injured his foot and that Elfin Dance had accepted only her to care for him? Or did Mr. Bonhumeur have big plans for them? He had mentioned both Antonia and his daughter, right? No, no. Antonia couldn't even entertain the thought of keeping Elfin Dance on the farm.

Then, suddenly, Maria came out of the office and asked Antonia about her riding qualification level. She also wanted to know exactly which awards, big and little, Antonia had already won in competitions.

"Even the ones when I was a little kid?" Antonia was just trying to be funny.

"Maybe, so that they can see you're a natural."

"That's not true."

"No, you are. But the last ones are the most important."

"What do you need them for?"

Maria gave her no answer.

So Antonia listed her awards, and Maria just nodded. Evidently she already had everything on her slip of paper. After that she scurried back into the office.

A little while later, the office door opened, and Antonia tried to tell from all their faces what direction the discussion had taken.

Maria had barely laid eyes on Antonia when she

rushed over to her, took her in her arms, and whispered in her ear, "Everything is absolutely marvelous! Merveilleuse." She laughed.

What was that supposed to mean? That Mr. Bonhumeur wouldn't take his horses back to France?

Antonia looked at all of them and yelled impatiently, "Don't keep us in suspense! Is Elfin Dance staying here for a while?"

Mr. Bonhumeur smiled and said, "My dear girl, Antonia, I would be very pleased eef you would take care of Elfin Dance. Cascara weel go to my daughter Juliette. You two weel get to know each ozzer, I promise. Per'aps one time or anozzer, you can train togezzer during zuh next vacation. You boz have talent, real talent."

Antonia couldn't believe her ears. What had Mr. Bonhumeur just said?

Then Papa repeated it. "You heard right, Antonia. Mr. Bonhumeur is leaving Elfin Dance and Asseem here. He's extending the contract under the condition that you care for and ride Elfin Dance, and that Mr. Hegemann gives you a lesson once a week from now on. Mr. Hegemann agreed immediately. Mr. Sonnenfeld, along with Caroline, will take care of Asseem and will also take on the rest of your riding lessons. What do you think?"

What did she think? To be trained by Hegemann? She couldn't believe it.

First she threw her arms around her father's neck. Then she gave Mr. Bonhumeur a big kiss on the cheek, and finally she ran with Leona to the stable to Elfin Dance and Snow White. They had to hear the news too. Snow White snorted contentedly and watched Antonia and Elfin Dance.

Elfin Dance shook his head, as though he had to let the news sink in first. Finally he nodded. Obviously everything had gone according to his plan.

"You're staying here, and we'll both get training. The best training in the world, from a famous show jumper. Imagine that!" Antonia pressed her head against Elfin Dance's neck. Slowly she began to understand what it all meant, for her, for the farm, and for her whole family.

Then Maria entered with Mr. Bonhumeur.

She stood up proudly in front of Antonia. "Now our Antonia will become a wonderful rider and jumper." At that moment, Elfin Dance reared and whinnied loudly—a whoop of delight!

"'Ee ees glad," said Mr. Bonhumeur. "'Ee feels comfortable weez Antonia. And zuh two of zem weell win many prizes. Elfin Dance and Antonia, zuh 'orse whisperer."